bits in a basket

By Tass Two Crows Flying, Medicine Woman
As told to Dr Zizz

with illustrations dreamed by Anya Kotzuba

dedications

Dr Zizz: For my father. With thanks to Ungini, the Absolute for the title and inspiration. And to Miranda, for your love and support.

Tass Two Crows Flying: Blessed daughters, Petra and Farrah — you inspired me to tell stories from when you were children.
Ainsley, for your unwavering belief that my words should be printed.

Anya Kotzuba: For myself, and thanks to Gary V for his incredible support and insight.

Handmade Life is a South African publishing company committed to the equitable sharing of profits with authors.

Layout, typesetting, logo and design by **Chip Snaddon**: chipsnaddon.porfoliobox.net

Images scanned by Artisanink: www.artisanink.co.za

Printed by: Print on Demand (PTY) Ltd
www.printondemand.co.za

ISBN : 978-0-620-91662-2

More at drzizz.com

bookend

The Author:

It began with Ceremony, both times. The beginning of a friendship on a Medicine walk.
Then that beach day of Transformation Ceremony,
when the story crawled out, and your pink pen began this journey.
Anemones waving. Your listening ears. Weaving.
Poetry spoken into your safe heart hands.

The Curator:

Every time we make a book, I realise all over again it's an act of love going out into the world, just like a person

Let me start with the trees.

I'll start with a Cedar,

The Evergreen of Life.

All trees are sacred,

take off your shoes.

I'll start with the trees,

old friends.

The Oaks,

the Coral Trees,

Plum

and Magnolia.

Compassionate survivors.

I'll start with the trees, the trees teach us,

as the Crow teaches.

Some people are cat people and some are dog people,

I've always been a crow person.

Sitting in a tree,

flying,

you know.

A feathered person.

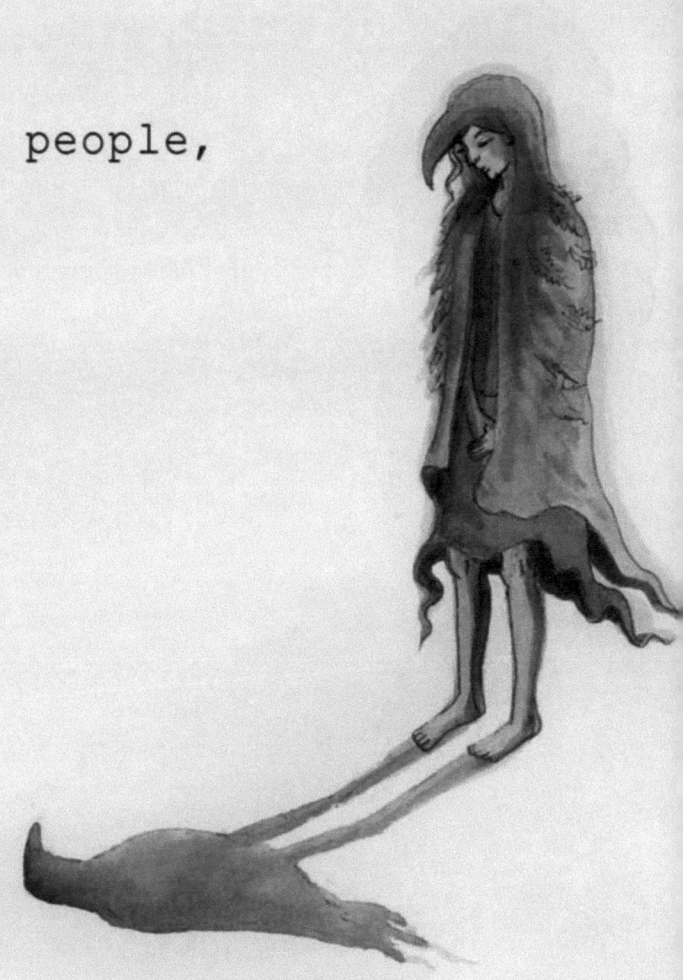

Now the wind's come up,

   it's a different language.

It's rich,

it's underground,

it's subterranean,

it's forbidden.

We are strong,

we grow no matter where you put us.

In between the spaces of death

there are gardens and regrowth.

But today I'm carrying a rough edge like an emery board,

scraping through the day.

I'm on the weird edge of me,

like lemons.

I been watching you,

you been odd.

It's a horrid tatty blanket
that I'm weaving.

Somedays it's a magic carpet,

but today all my bits come off

like ribbons streaming out of me.

Coyote energy.

I've been the victim of myself.

I'm a mess,

Sisters, can you help me?

Sometimes we're the basket,

that's a very well-woven feeling.

But when we're of the stuff inside,

that's where we find our real humanity,

the sum total of ourselves.

A yarn of wool, a dead fish.

The mouldy stuff at the back of the fridge.

Here is my habit of misery,

of fear,

my parasite:

"I'm living in you, baby!"

Not today, you're not.

Speak to them in German if you must.

Then it is most frightening and true.

Get out, RAUS!

Your narrative of half-woman:

flush it down the toilet,

dance around it,

light a candle,

do SOMETHING!

Dive right in and dive right out.

Make a shift,

don't swim in it.

Wallow is not a good energy.

Wallowing in a toilet is especially bad.

That's where shapeshifters drown.

Yes, I know.

You don't know till you know

and then you find out things

in strange ways sometimes.

Just   stay   with   me.

And here we are, having a no-curtains conversation.

If you saw me today

you would have seen mountains, streams, rivers

and flocks of crows

streaming from my mouth.

The ocean is roaring in my power centre.

I am feeding myself in unimaginable ways.

A forest of fruit trees.

Wildness, carrying tomatoes.

Shining in the shade.

Last night you were rustling,

today you're still as a pond.

I love you in all weathers.

Like birth:

Here I go,

with the utmost fortitude

into the ultimate uncertainty.

Watch my hand,

pick the finger.

The paper is trees,

this book is my transformation ceremony.

I am flagrantly myself,

Irrepressible.

bookend

The Artist:

This book has had an energy of its own, a deep magic that flowed through it
as the words and my own journey synchronised in a dark night of the soul.
I shed tears and connected to my strength through the process of painting the story.
A new beginning: the birth of my heart art. It has been an inspiring and beautiful experience.